Let's Play Tag!

Read the Page

Say It   Sound It   Spell It

Game

Repeat

Stop

Why is wh yellow?

Yellow highlights represent letter teams that make a single sound or words with irregular decoding patterns.

The Bike Race

Story by Holly Melton
Illustrated by Tom Pansini and Darryl Goudreau

 Lily and Leap were on a hike. They saw a sign.
"Look! A bike race!" said Leap. "I think I'll ride in it."

"I'll ride in it, too!"
said Lily.
Leap said, "You are
only five. You don't
know how to ride
a bike."
"You are almost nine.
Teach me!" said Lily.

 "I can fix this bike," said Leap. "These small wheels are nice. But it's time to take them off!"

Tad rode up on his trike. "I like your bike," he said. "Can I ride with you?" Lily said, "Let's go!"

📖 Leap ran beside Lily. He held the bike. Then he let go.

Things were not fine
anymore! Lily almost
ran into a pine tree.
She almost hit
a slide.

 "Use your brakes!" said Leap. Lily did not use her brakes. Her bike tire hit a pile of rocks. She fell off her bike.

Lily put ice on her knee. She did not whine or cry.
But Tad was mad.
"Bad, bad bike!"

Lily got back on her bike. She fell once. She fell twice. She got back on her bike again.

"Try one more time!"
said Leap. "You can
do it!"
This time, Lily did
not fall!

 "Look at me, I can ride!" said Lily. Tad said, "Good, good bike."

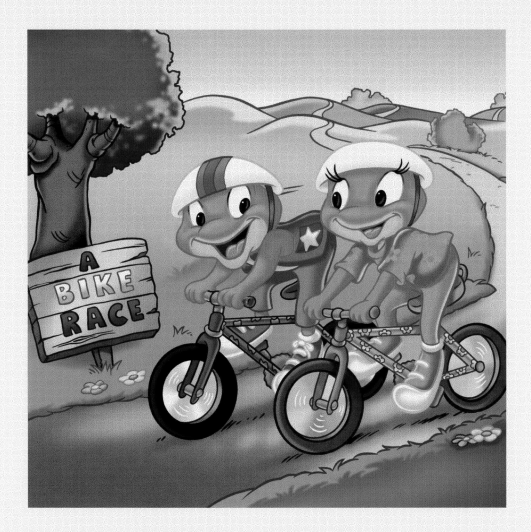

Lily said, "The race is tomorrow. I want to be ready." She rode for a long time.

It was time for the race. "Line up your bikes!" said the starter. "You will race for five miles. Ready, set, go!"

Leap was very fast.
"I will win a prize!"
he thought. He gave
a wave to Lily.

📖 Leap's tire hit a
nail. The tire went
pop! Leap fell into
a pile of dirt.
"Oh, no! A flat
tire!" he said.

"Are you okay?"
asked Lily.
"I'm fine," said Leap.
"Don't stop Lily!
You still have time
to win a prize!"

 Lily gave a smile. "A prize would be nice," she said. "But maybe some other time. Now, we have a tire to fix!"

Leap and Lily fixed
the flat tire. Many
bikes went by.
"It's fixed. Let's
go!" said Leap.

Leap and Lily rode across the line. They were side by side. Tad said "Hooray! Do you get a prize for last place?"

Lily gave a big smile.
She said, "What
a great day! I got
to ride five miles.
I learned how to fix
a flat tire!"

Tad said, "I am a big boy. I am too big for a trike. I bet I can ride a bike. Here I go!"

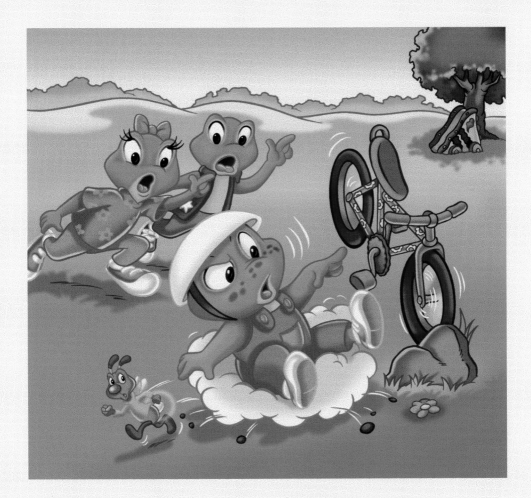

"Tad, no!" said Lily.
"Stop!" said Leap. They
ran after the bike.
"Bad bike! Bad bike!"
said Tad.

"Are you okay, Tad?" asked Lily. Tad said, "Your bike is nice. But I like mine better. A trike is the bike for me!"

Activities

dim   dime

Tim   time

slim   slime

rip   ripe

kit   kite

pin   pine

1. prize

2. hive

3. fin

4. ride

5. bit

6. grip

7. slide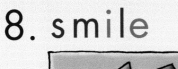

8. smile

Words You're Learning
Long Vowels, Silent E & Y

Long i_e Words

bike	miles	pine
fine	mine	ride
five	nice	side
hike	nine	time
ice	pile	tire
line		

Long a_e Words

brakes
make
race
take
wave

Sight Words

a	for	is	they	what
again	have	put	very	would
are	here	said	were	you
do	I	the		

Challenging Words

across	dirt	other	slide	trike
almost	fall	place	small	try
anymore	flat	prize	smile	twice
asked	great	ready	stop	wheels
behind	Leap	rocks	teach	whine
beside	learned	shine	thought	
cry	nail	sign	tomorrow	